Lovable Liam

Affirmations for a Perfectly Imperfect Child

Jane Whelen Banks

Jessica Kingsley Publishers
London and Philadelphia

First published in 2009
by Jessica Kingsley Publishers
116 Pentonville Road
London N1 9JB, UK
and
400 Market Street, Suite 400
Philadelphia, PA 19106, USA

www.jkp.com

Library of Congress Cataloging in Publication Data
Banks, Jane Whelen.
  Loveable Liam : affirmations for a perfectly imperfect child / Jane Whelen Banks.
     p. cm.
  ISBN 978-1-84310-899-3 (hb : alk. paper)
  1. Love--Juvenile literature. I. Title.
  BF575.L8B235 2009
  155.4'18--dc22

                              2008017640

British Library Cataloguing in Publication Data
A CIP catalogue record for this book is available from the British Library

ISBN 978 1 84310 899 3

Printed and bound in China by
Reliance Printing Co, Ltd.

Dedication

To Jamie, Morgon and Liam,
my perfectly imperfect children.

All young children require direction. They require discipline and boundaries, education, and rewards. As parents, we teach manners, traditions, morality, and social conduct. It is through our guidance that we prepare our children for a social world. However, the addition of speech therapy, behavior modification, social skills classes, and occupational therapy (to name a few), while necessary to some children's development, may also reinforce a sense of brokenness. In spite of our good intentions our actions may risk eroding a tender ego. **Lovable Liam** takes a moment to honor a child for who he is. As spoken words are seldom enough, **Lovable Liam** attempts to ensure, through visual examples, that Liam is a wonderful and precious child, who is deeply valued amongst his friends and adored by his family.

This is Liam.

Liam is a wonderful kid, with lots of
friends and family who love him.

Liam is lovable because he shares his toys nicely with others. Once he let Trevor take home his favorite backhoe.

Liam is lovable because he always asks politely when he wants to borrow his friends' stuff.

And he always says, "Thanks a lot," when his friends lend him their belongings.

Liam is gracious when kids don't want to share their toys with him. He does not pester them, or hoard his own toys to "get even."

Liam is lovable because he is kind
and gentle with animals.

Babies love Liam too, because he talks
and smiles at them and makes them feel special.
Once he made Meredith stop crying when
he made funny faces at her.

Liam is lovable because he has a great laugh and is lots of fun to play with. He takes turns on the slide and doesn't push...much.

Liam is lovable because he is honest. He tells people how he feels. He doesn't throw things or hit others.

Liam is lovable because he shows you how happy he is to see you. He makes his Mommy and Daddy feel great with his big cuddly hugs and smoochie kisses.

Liam is lovable even when he whines and won't eat his dinner. He can be annoying, but he is still lovable.

When people are cross with Liam, they still love him. Being cross will only last for a little while. Love will last forever.

There are so many reasons why Liam is lovable. Happy or sad, sharing or stingy, laughing or whining, Liam is just right the way he is, and we all love him.

Liam, you are so lovable!